The Brontë Sisters
Quiz and Puzzle Book

by
Maggie
Lane

Abson Books   Abson   Wick   Bristol

For my own Emily Charlotte

ABSON BOOKS, Abson, Wick, Bristol, England
First published in Great Britain, April 1983.

© Maggie Lane
Design: Paul Lane. Artwork: Mike Flanders.
Typesetting: Gina Shepperd

ISBN 0 902920 51 0
Printed at the Burleigh Press, Bristol, England.

Introduction

All the puzzles and quizzes contained in this book have been inspired by the seven completed novels of the three Brontë sisters; all the answers are to be found somewhere in the pages of Anne's 'Agnes Grey' or 'The Tenant of Wildfell Hall', Emily's 'Wuthering Heights', or Charlotte's 'Jane Eyre', 'Shirley', 'Villette' or 'The Professor'.

There are twelve **Quizzes** designed to challenge your memory of such details as Clothes, Colours, Relations, Occupations, Cookery, Christmas, Villages, Seasons, Dates, Interiors and Flowers as depicted in the works of the Brontës.

Then there are the **Name Games,** one for each novel. By fitting the names of the major characters into the empty squares, reading across, the name of a further character from the same novel will appear between the bold lines, reading down. Please note that a full point marks the division between two component parts of any character's name.

Each **Crossword Puzzle** in this book is devoted to one Brontë novel, the clues consisting entirely of quotations from that work. First decide from the evidence in the clues which is the novel concerned; then supply the missing word from each quotation to solve the crossword puzzle.

There are also four **Word Search Puzzles** - on the themes of Pets, Pupils, Servants and Houses. In each case, names from the given category have been concealed in a grid of letters; they may read horizontally, vertically or diagonally, backwards or forwards, and letters may be used more than once, or not at all. One word has been picked out already to start you off on each puzzle; as you locate the others, draw around them on the grid, and at the same time list them in the space on the page until the specified number of words has been discovered.

Finally, you are invited to guess which are the characters portrayed in the **Illustrations;** to make it a little bit harder, the name of the novel illustrated is not disclosed. Reproduced by kind permission of J M Dent & Sons Ltd, these charming drawings are by Edmund Dulac for an Edwardian edition of the Brontë novels.

Answers to all the quizzes and puzzles are given at the back of this book - but I suspect that Brontë lovers will prefer to pore over the novels themselves until the last elusive reference has been tracked down. Indeed, one of the pleasures for me in devising the following pages has been rereading the complete Brontë canon paying particular attention to detail. The compelling quality of the Brontë storytelling is conducive to racing ahead - even Thackeray stayed up all night to finish 'Jane Eyre' - caring desperately as one does for the characters, and longing to know what befalls them. Subsequent readings can reveal, not only many insights missed the first or even second time around, but a wealth of quiet detail which builds up to give solidity to those remarkable sisters' hauntingly imaginative world.

Happy puzzling! M.L.

Word Search

Houses

Concealed in the grid are the names of 19 country houses from the novels of the Brontë sisters. 15 of the names have two components; the remainder are single words. Encircle the answers on the grid and list them in the space below. The first has been done for you.

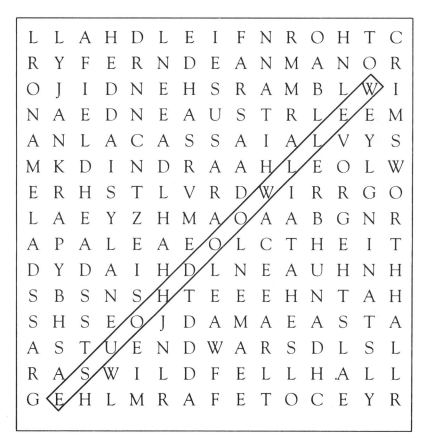

```
L L A H D L E I F N R O H T C
R Y F E R N D E A N M A N O R
O J I D N E H S R A M B L W I
N A E D N E A U S T R L E E M
A N L A C A S S A I A L V Y S
M K D I N D R A A H L E O L W
E R H S T L V R D W I R R G O
L A E Y Z H M A O A A B G N R
A P A L E A E O L C T H E I T
D Y D A I H D L N E A U H N H
S B S N S H T E E E H N T A H
S H S E O J D A M A E A S T A
A S T U E N D W A R S D L S L
R A S W I L D F E L L H A L L
G E H L M R A F E T O C E Y R
```

Name Game 1

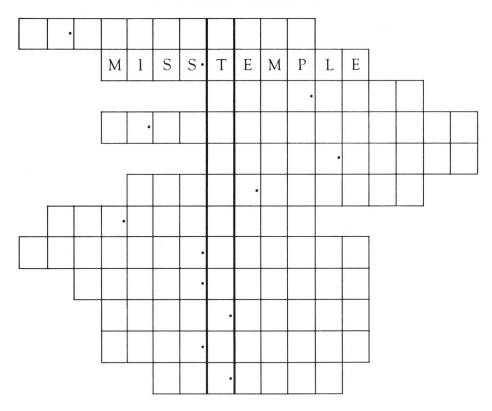

The grid contains the name: M I S S · T E M P L E

Couples

Match the bride and groom

1	Diana Rivers	A	Sir Thomas Ashby
2	Esther Hargrave	B	Jack Halford
3	Ginevra Fanshawe	C	Captain Fitzjames
4	Dora Sykes	D	Robert Leaven
5	Rose Markham	E	Alfred de Hamal
6	Maria Temple	F	Davy Sweeting
7	Zoraide Reuter	G	Frederick Lawrence
8	Rosalie Murray	H	Francois Pelet
9	Helen Hattersley	I	Rev. Mr Nasmyth
10	Bessie Lee	J	Arthur Huntingdon jnr

Across

1 and 1 Down "As different as moonbeam from lightning, or ... from ... " (5,4)

3 Eager to partake in the ... of the hearth (6)

7 Laden with oatcakes and clusters of legs of beef, mutton and ... (3)

9 Unquiet slumbers for sleepers in that quiet ... (5)

12 I set his plate to keep warm on the ... (6)

13 A curl of light hair, fastened with a silver ... (6)

16 "... were quarrelling like cats about you" (2)

17 "You'd better let the dog ..." (5)

19 "Shall regret and repent it till I ...!" (3)

21 He is a dark skinned ... aspect (5)

23 'I shudder ... you" (2)

24 A paved ... containing a coal-shed, pump and pigeon-cote (4)

26 Sent me a ... expressing her sorrow (6)

28 "They wouldn't let me go to the ... of the garden-wall" (3)

29 He told Zillah to give ... a glass of brandy (2)

Down

1 See 1 Across
2 Shame and pride threw a double gloom ... his countenance (4)
3 "I've been a ... for twenty years" (4)
4 "Nelly, I ... Heathcliff" (2)
5 A few ... books, piled up in one corner (8)
6 "You and Edgar have broken my ... " (5)
8 "..., mamma, mamma!" (2)
10 I stirred up the ... and interred them under a shovel full of coals (5)
11 The clergyman's stipend is only ... pounds per annum (6)
14 Beholding such a bright, graceful ... (6)
15 Our mutual ... (3)
18 "Not even a rabbit, or a weasel's ...?" (4)
20 An immense fire, compounded of coal, ... and wood (4)
21 She rose in high ..., eager to join her cousin (4)
22 "Two candles on the table making the black press shine like ... (3)
23 Pinched me very spitefuly on the ... (3)
25 "Weather-bound for half ... hour" (2)
27 A sky too dappled and hazy ... threaten rain (2)

9

Dates

Name the date of the month on which

1   The Markhams held a party
_____

2   M. Paul celebrated his fête
_____

3   Polly Home was born
_____

4   Aunt Julienne Henri died
_____

5   Helen Lawrence began her diary
_____

6   Jane Eyre travelled to Lowood
_____

7   Rosalie Murray made her debut in society
_____

8   Sir Thomas Ashby married
_____

9   The Huntingdons first quarrelled
_____

10   Mr Brocklehurst visited Mrs Reed
_____

Relations

What was the Christian name of

1   Caroline Helston's uncle
_____

2   Helen Huntingdon's aunt
_____

3   Bertha Rochester's father
_____

4   Mr Brocklehurst's mother
_____

5   William Crimsworth's son
_____

6   Agnes Grey's husband
_____

7   Blanche Ingram's brother
_____

8   Rose Yorke's sister
_____

9   Mr Wilmot's niece
_____

10   Lucy Snowe's godmother
_____

Word Search

Pets

Concealed in the grid are the names of 27 pets from the novels of the Brontë sisters: 18 dogs, 8 horses and one cat. Encircle the answers on the grid and list them in the space below. The first has been done for you.

```
S  S  E  B  K  C  A  L  B  E  N  R  Y  T  G
A  H  O  D  M  A  X  I  N  E  O  H  P  N  R
N  S  A  F  R  A  E  N  C  I  S  H  A  W  I
C  S  S  K  U  L  K  E  R  I  O  S  L  L  M
H  Y  R  I  A  M  R  C  H  E  H  A  R  L  A
O  L  U  E  F  L  O  W  B  E  S  P  G  E  L
O  V  O  R  G  E  Y  E  R  P  R  H  I  M  K
O  I  R  I  S  N  L  N  A  I  E  U  D  O  I
N  E  S  E  N  L  P  H  N  I  I  A  B  T  N
U  I  E  I  A  P  R  C  L  A  I  D  E  Y  R
J  A  M  N  P  D  E  R  P  R  F  O  E  E  A
J  U  D  R  I  I  A  C  E  E  Z  J  M  R  T
M  A  E  A  O  H  L  M  N  S  F  A  I  G  R
E  L  D  P  C  D  A  O  L  R  A  C  R  K  A
R  E  L  T  T  O  R  H  T  S  R  K  E  N  T
```

Name Game 2

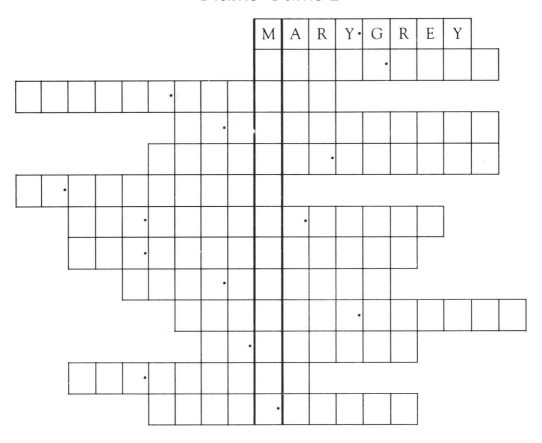

Flowers

1 What clothed the library window at Daisy Lane

2 Which flower did Caroline Helstone preserve in her pocket-book

3 Among the leaves and bells of which wild flowers did the young Jane Eyre look for elves

4 What blossom did Zoraide Reuter pluck for William Crimsworth

5 Which wild flowers did Helen Huntingdon instruct her son to gather

6 What did Agnes Grey press between the leaves of her bible

7 Which flower reminded Catherine Linton of soft thaw winds, warm sunshine and nearly melted snow

8 What cut flowers lent fragrance to the parlour at 7 Faubourg Clotilde

9 In 1802, which two garden flowers scented the air at Wuthering Heights

10 Which four conservatory plants were watered by M. Paul

Across

1. England - that dear land of … (5)
4. On the walls hung two … (4)
7. Its own more solemn … (3)
9. I forgot that there were fields, woods, …, seas (6)
10. This food was limited to coffee and … (4)
12. In this … gown of shadow, I felt at home (4)
14. To me she commented … more on her lover's beauty (2)
18. Inhaling the … of baked apples afar (9)
20. Pere Silas dropped … hints (4)
21. The increasing … and gathering gloom (5)
22. Guiltless of flounce … furbelow (2)
24. My … lived in a handsome house (9)
26. I dried the violets; kept them, and have them … (5)
27. Black was the river … a torrent of ink (2)
28. Presently I found myself in Paternoster … (3)

1 "Where Miss Fanshawe is concerned, you … no respect" (5)

2 That storm roared frenzied for … days (5)

3 "I seem to live in a … of moral antipodes (4)

4 … little morsel of human affection (2)

5 "You shall mind your health and happiness for my …" (4)

6 "Yes, … was kind on Sundays" (2)

8 … had reached the middle of a clean faubourg (2)

10 "The most peculiar, … little woman he knows" (10)

11 "I … going to school" (2)

13 To … meaning from my eyes, vision from the page (5)

15 The ghostly nun … the garden (2)

16 Softened by some drapery of black … (4)

17 "Pink or …, yellow or crimson, pea-green or sky-blue" (7)

19 My work had … charm for my taste, nor hold on my interest (7)

20 "Shall I …?" was her question (2)

23 "That mighty … in wood and wax, and kid and satin" (4)

25 The leaden gloom of … and blustering autumn (3)

Name Game 3

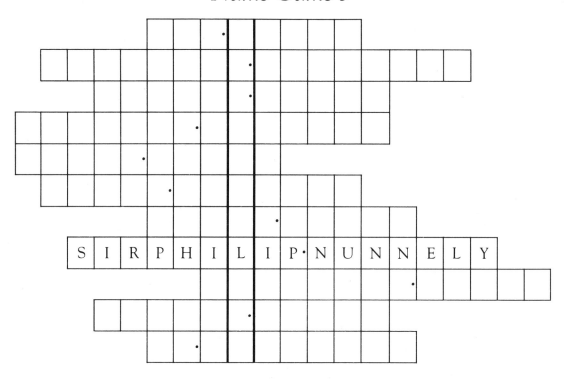

Christmas

1 Who stipulated for a Christmas holiday before engaging herself as a governess

2 Who sang carols to herself on Christmas Eve

3 In which house was 'Old England' toasted with a Christmas wassail cup of hot spiced ale

4 Who visited the sick and poor every day although it was Christmas week

5 In which year did fifteen instruments play Christmas music at Wuthering Heights

6 At Christmas parties, who wore thin muslin frocks and scarlet sashes, with hair elaborately ringletted

7 In which house was the clock decked with Christmas holly

8 Who plucked a Christmas rose

9 How much did old Mr Earnshaw habitually give Ellen Dean as a Christmas box

10 Whose fiancé died on Christmas Day

Across

1 "I was told," said he, "that you were a perfect …, Miss Grey" (8)

6 "I'll leave you at the … of the next street" (3)

8 "Fine, bold, …, mischievous boys" (6)

9 "Carrying … and bone soup to her husband's poor parishioners" (6)

11 At sixteen, Miss Murray was something of a … (4)

12 "They are clever children, and very apt to …" (5)

13 The deep, clear azure of the sky and the … (5)

15 "A usurper, a tyrant, an incubus, a … " (3)

17 "I have nothing but … to complain of" (8)

21 It came like a thunder-clap on … all (2)

22 I defy anyone to blame him … a pastor, a husband or a father (2)

23 Made my father smile again, … sadly (4;)

24 … sweet evening towards the close of May (3)

25 To conceal my …, I buried my face in my hands (7)

1 … were numbered among my favourite flowers (9)
2 … clothes were mended, turned and darned (3)
3 A wide, white … was all that met my gaze (10)
4 Divided her time between the Continent and the … (10)
5 "We will take a few young ladies to board and … (10)
7 The tangled seaweed and the … rocks beneath (6)
0 "Weighing her … purse against her faded charms" (5)
4 "I must be a prisoner … a slave" (3)
6 "Will she wear a white apron, and make … and puddings?" (4)
8 "I lost the … and dearest of my early friends" (4)
9 Who ever hung his hopes … so frail a twig? (4)
0 "Not … to escape the infamy of old maidenhood" (4)
1 Why so much beauty should be given to those who make so bad a … of it (3)

Name Game 4

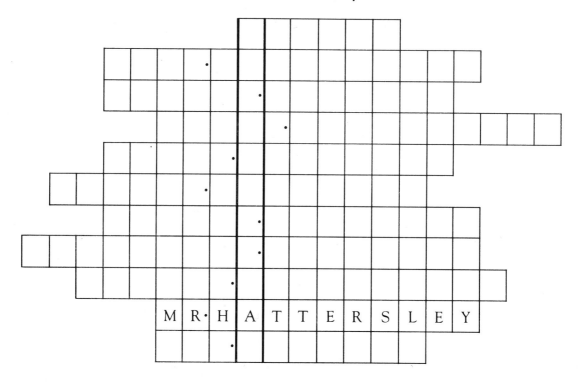

M R·H A T T E R S L E Y

Clothes

Who wore

1 Brown stuff frocks and long holland pinafores

2 A ball dress of white gauze over pink satin

3 A scarlet shawl and black silk bonnet

4 A mackintosh

5 A nun's habit

6 A red cloak and a broad-brimmed gypsy hat tied down with a striped hankerchief

7 A wrapping-gown, shawl and soundless slippers

8 A purple dress with a Spanish trimming of black and a gold watch at her girdle

9 A stuff petticoat, striped cotton camisole, and curl-papers

10 A blue morocco collar

Across

1 "Take her away to the …, and lock her in there" (3-4)
5 Twenty thousand pounds shared equally, would b
    five thousand … (4)
7 "I have my petition … ready" (3)
8 "Any ill …?" I demanded (4)
9 Splendidly attired in velvet, silk and … (4)
10 "I … not stay any longer" (4)
11 "The veil, torn from top … bottom in two halves!"
    (2)
13 "I am your plain, Quakerish …" (9)
17 "My pint of porter and bit of pudding … a tray" (2)
18 "He has a fine … voice" (4)
20 The growth of … or some other creeping plant (3)
21 "There has been a fire; … up, do" (3)
22 The volume was flung, it … me, and I fell (3)
24 What other bridegroom ever looked as … did (2)
25 "… and Mr Rochester sang a duet" (3)
26 "You think too much of the love of … beings" (5)
29 "Cold as an …" (7)
30 "Mrs Reed kept the orphan … years" (3)
31 "The battle is fought and the victory …" (3)

Down

1 ..., I married him (6)
2 "You are less than a servant, for you ... nothing for your keep" (2)
3 "To endure ... more night under this roof" (3)
4 "God bless you, my dear ... " (6)
5 "It was a fairy, and came from ... land" (3)
6 "Julia's hair ... naturally" (5)
8 "Make a little hot ... and cut a sandwich or two" (5)
2 "Whether gown, sheet ... shroud, I cannot tell" (2)
4 "I have ... kindred to interfere" (2)
5 No charm powerful enough to solve the ..." (6)
6 "A look and air at once ... and independent" (3)
8 "Fresh as the wild honey the ... gathers on the moor" (3)
9 "... once so frail and so indomitable" (2)
1 "She started as if she had seen a ... " (5)
2 A handful of ... and blossoms to put in a coffin (5)
3 Many old .. trees, strong, knotty and broad as oaks (5)
7 When morning had advanced to ... (4)
8 "We may neither think nor talk lightly without ..." (3)

Colours

What was the colour of

1 The carpet at Thrushcross Grange

2 The chintz bedroom curtains at Thornfield

3 Mrs Bretton's tea service

4 Joseph's quilt

5 Jane Eyre's gingham dress

6 The dress Lucy's godmother gave her

7 Adele's satin sandals

8 Madame Beck's hair

9 The silk purse Zoraide Reuter was netting

10 The schoolroom carpet at Wellwood

Word Search

Pupils

Concealed in the grid are the Christian names of 29 pupils from the novels of the Brontë sisters: 25 girls and 4 boys. Encircle the answers on the grid and list them in the space below. The first has been done for you.

```
E  I  L  A  S  O  R  M  A  G  S  G  I  N  S
I  U  E  M  A  R  Y  A  N  N  E  C  E  E  E
N  L  L  L  O  N  A  N  E  A  R  A  M  L  C
I  E  A  E  R  T  N  G  A  I  O  T  N  E  N
G  N  R  O  L  A  R  A  R  L  L  H  L  H  A
R  I  E  N  T  I  B  A  U  U  O  E  T  O  R
I  L  N  I  E  A  E  N  A  J  D  R  R  R  F
V  O  P  E  I  L  A  E  U  A  T  I  Q  T  A
W  R  Y  J  V  I  U  L  B  K  R  N  H  E  D
P  A  Z  K  L  R  E  L  O  G  C  E  P  N  L
H  C  H  E  Y  S  A  E  L  L  E  B  A  S  I
V  Y  R  N  S  N  Y  W  O  J  Z  A  G  E  T
X  U  N  I  C  H  A  R  L  E  S  P  N  A  A
A  A  B  H  Y  W  T  H  A  R  R  I  E  T  M
F  B  E  U  Q  I  L  E  G  N  A  X  S  U  Q
```

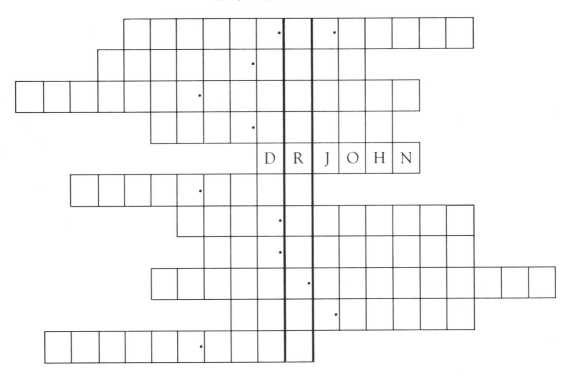

D R J O H N

Cookery

1 Who put too much pepper in a pie

2 What did Mr Malone cook on Robert Moore's gridiron

3 What had Ellen Dean been cutting with the carving knife

4 When Lucy Snowe visited her old nurse, what did she find her cooking

5 What type of soup did Hortense Moore make

6 The cookery of which dish did Isabella take over from Joseph

7 What was Mary cooking when she heard of Jane's marriage to Rochester

8 Who cooked Yorkshire pudding for three curates

9 Where were eggs beaten, currants sorted and spices grated

10 Who received a gift of home-made currant jam

Across

2 The … sun was gleaming redly on the old hall (9)
6 "In seven years more, I shall be … tall as you" (2)
7 "It is a secret … you meditate!" (6)
8 My mother's maiden … was Graham (4)
9 "I cannot believe there is any … in those laughing blue eyes" (4)
10 "Give … my flesh and blood lover!" (2)
11 I pursued the even tenor of … way (2)
12 "My heart is too thoroughly … to be broken" (5)
15 "Always did justice … my good dinners" (2)
16 "A … affections should never be won unsought" (5
17 You must … back with me to the autumn of 1827 (
18 A light wind swept over the … (4)
20 Their … against the hapless partridges (10)
24 Gone to … with a slight attack of the gout (3)

1 My ... materials were laid together (8)
2 His idea of a ... is a thing to love one devotedly and to stay at home (4)
3 "Rose, don't put so many ... in the pudding" (6)
4 "I would ... run away with the butler" (6)
5 "A sweet, wild rosebud ... with dew" (6)
? "Nobody dead? Nobody ...?" (7)
? "Gilbert, ... leave me," she cried (2)
? All the ... vices a little child can show (6)
? "Very anxious to see ... all well married" (2)
? "Cupid's arrows have been ... sharp for you" (3)
? Detected some ... hairs among his beloved chestnut locks (4)
? Seated at the chimney-corner, with the ... on her knee (3)
? "You are going to ... me of my niece" (3)
   and 22 " ... ... a woman's nature to be constant" (2,2)
? "I thought there would ... good come of it" (2)

Name Game 6

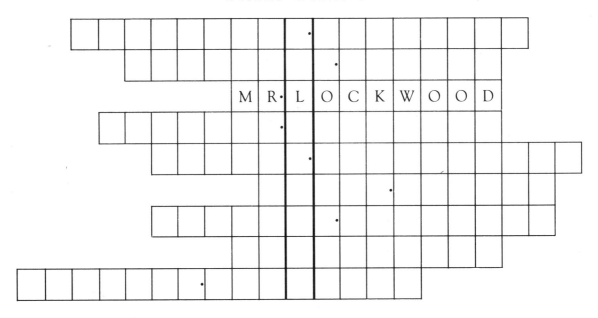

M R · L O C K W O O D

Seasons

1 Which season bred pestilence at Lowood

6 Which season did Helen Huntingdon refuse to consider for her second wedding day

2 Following.which quarter-day did Edgar Linton catch a fatal chill

7 What comforted Lucy Snowe when a north wind cast a blight over Europe

3 Where did Adele gather wild strawberries on Midsummer Eve

8 Which crop was harvested three weeks later at Gimmerton than elsewhere in the county

4 At which time of the church calendar was a school feast organisd at Briarfield

9 Which book was delivered to Gilbert Markham as he was busy haymaking

5 Who spent his autumnal vacation on a pilgrimage to Rome

10 Which book was Jane Eyre reading when St John Rivers came in out of a snow storm

Across

1 "Can ... alone make a human being happy?" (6)
5 "They want caning . ... boys!" (3)
7 "You will be restricted to ... milk and Yorkshire oatcake" (3)
9 "Only three ... : his niece and two servants" (5)
10 "I have neither ..., pain nor fever" (5)
12 Flogged a son of his own for telling a ... (3)
13 The contrary gift of turning ... to stone (4)
14 "My good aunt and my ... cousins" (5)
15 "Do the counting-house work, ... the books, and write the letters" (4)
18 "She was a wild, ... thing, but pleasant to have in the room" (8)
21 A native of the ... of shamrocks and potatoes (4)
22 "I wear a high dress ... a collar" (3)
25 "Potent as a ..., and brave as a lion" (5)
27 "His secrecy ... me" (5)
28 "The ... and young should hold the opinions of th cool and middle-aged" (5)

Down

1 "You are a ... little person, Caroline" (8)
2 "You must give me a ... of pistols" (5)
3 "Affection, like love, will be ... now and then" (6)
4 "With light and ... she woos the primrose from the turf" (3)
6 "I have been in sad pain, and ..., and misery" (6)
8 "I often wonder what I came into the ... for" (5)
11 "He felt no obligation to treat me with ..." (6)
16 "Exact what ... you will" (6)
17 "Your most faithful prop in ..." (3)
19 Fetch a chaise from the Red House ... (3)
20 "She has her books for a pleasure, and her brother for a ..." (4)
22 Though the beef was 'tough' they ... a great deal of it (3)
23 "I shall enquire whether the ... was really mad" (3)
24 "She walked nearly as ... as Nunnely" (3)
26 "She ... very vague and visionary" (2)

33

Occupations

What was the occupation of

1 Celine Valens

2 Mr Kenneth

3 Frances Henri

4 Sir George Lynn

5 M. Miret

6 John Gale

7 Timothy Ramsden

8 Zelie St Pierre

9 Cyril Hall

10 Mr Briggs

Villages

In which town or village did

1 Jane Eyre keep school

2 Mr Hatfield hold the living

3 William Crimsworth decline the living

4 Robert Moore go to market

5 Edgar Linton marry

6 Helen Burns have her home

7 Helen 'Graham' sketch

8 Mr Rochester choose two dresses

9 St John Rivers catch the coach

10 Fanny buy muffins, crumpets and biscuits

Word Search

Servants

Concealed in the grid are the names of 32 servants from the novels of the Brontë sisters. 18 are known by their first name only, 7 by surname only, and a further 7 by both. Encircle the answers on the grid and list them in the space below. The first has been done for you.

```
Q M Y A N O S M A I L L I W R
D I T E L L E N D E A N N N E
Y S O P H I E J D A N O N A M
O N B J O S E P H A N N A H I
R O B E R T L E A V E N T Z C
T S A A S S E J S H W U W T H
A N A X J S O I B A R B A R A
G E H R E H I E R D M B R I E
R B T O N Y T E Z R E N R N L
U R R S N T R I L E A T E E M
M O A I Y L L A S E O H N T N
D W M N R L L A M N E D W T O
E N N E A L I C E W O O D E T
R A O H L O U I S O N O D H O
F A Z I L E L O O P E C A R G
```

Name Game 7

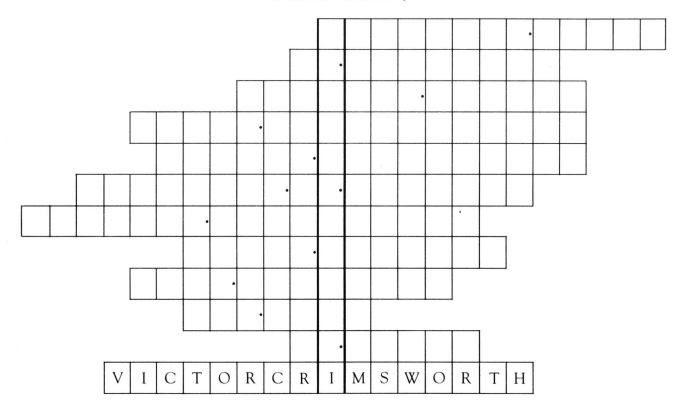

Interiors

Which room is described

1 A room where the first object that met the eye was a painter's easel, with a table beside it covered with rolls of canvas, bottles of oil and varnish, palette, brushes, paints etc.

2 A room with a sanded floor, clean scoured; a dresser of walnut, with pewter plates ranged in rows, reflecting the redness and radiance of a glowing peat fire

3 The chamber was a room shadowy with pale blue hangings, vaporous with curtainings and veilings of muslin; the bed semed to me like snowdrift and mist - spotless, soft and gauzy

4 A large, stately apartment, with purple chairs and curtains, a Turkey carpet, walnut panelled walls, one vast window rich in stained glass, and a lofty ceiling, nobly moulded

5 The whole furniture consisted of a chair, a clothes-press, and a large oak case, with squares cut out near the top, resembling coach windows

6 A place for business, with a bare, planked floor, a safe, two high desks and stools, and some chairs

7 An immense room with a fireplace at each end, a chandelier pendant from the ceiling, and a little red gallery high up against the wall filled with musical instruments

8 Its delicate walls were tinged like a blush; its floors were waxed; a square of brilliant carpet covered its centre; its small round table shone like the mirror over its hearth

Across

1 I loved her as she stood there, … and parentless (9)
5 Tales of adventure, … or wonder (5)
7 England is something … (6)
9 " … ambition especially, is not a feeling to be cherished" (8)
11 " … a wooden spoon will shovel up broth" (4)
14 "You can speak French - with a … English accent" (4)
16 In the library of my own home I … now writing (2)
17 "I have forgotten … of my gloves" (3)
18 By turns I … vivacity, vanity, coquetry (3)
20 "A drunken man is … match for a sober one" (2)
22 A … in the art of kissing (6)
24 As constant to the … as herself (6)
26 "Better … be without logic than without feeling" (2
28 The ripe grapes … the high trellis (2)
29 "Marrying a rich …, or running away with an heiress (5)
30 I served Edward as his second … faithfully (5)

1 "She is a … of mine - a Swiss girl" (5)
2 Neither brooch, ring … ribbon (3)
3 "God bless my little …!" (3)
4 There was a crescent … of moonlight (5)
6 "One of your uncles is a …" (4)
7 Belgium! name … and unpoetic (10)
8 "My country … the world" (2)
10 Women can love a downright ugly man if he
   be but … (8)
12 "The very morning after your … to me" (5)
13 Enthusiasm about a mere … (4)
14 "An old maid's life must doubtless be … and
   vapid (4)
15 Clad all .. white (2)
16 Happy … a bird with its mate (2)
19 Lost in a passion of the wildest … (3)
21 "The angel … the demon of my race" (2)
23 "Let me get to the fire, Mr Hunsden: I have
   something to … " (4)
25 Some thickly planted nursery of … and cypress (3)
27 … became a glutton of books (2)

Page

4 **ILLUSTRATION** Mr and Mrs Earnshaw, Hindley, Catherine, Heathcliff, Ellen Dean.

5 **WORD SEARCH: HOUSES (across)** Ferndean Manor, Wildfell Hall, Thornfield Hall, Ryecote Farm, Marsh End. **(down)** Grassdale Manor, Crimsworth Hall, Fieldhead, Ashby Park, Staningly, Daisy Lane, The Grove. **(diagonal)** Gateshead Hall, Wellwood House, Vale Hall, Briarmains, Linden Car, The Leas.

6 **NAME GAME 1** Mr Rochester, Miss Temple, Jane Eyre, Mr Brocklehurst, Helen Burns, Diana Rivers, Mrs Fairfax, Blanche Ingram, Adele Valens, Grace Poole, Mary Rivers, Mrs Reed. **(down)** St John Rivers.

7 **COUPLES** Diana Rivers m. Captain Fitzjames, Esther Hargraves m. Frederick Lawrence, Ginevra Fanshawe m. Alfred de Hamal, Dora Sykes m. Davy Sweeting, Rose Markham m. Jack Halford, Maria Temple m. Rev. Mr Nasmyth, Zoraide Reuter m. Francois Pelet, Rosalie Murray m. Sir Thomas Ashby, Helen Hattersley m. Arthur Huntingdon jnr, Bessie Lee m. Robert Leaven.

8 **ILLUSTRATION** Edward and William Crimsworth.

9 **WUTHERING HEIGHTS (across)** 1 Frost. 3 Warmth. 7 Ham. 9 Earth. 12 Fender. 13 Thread. 16 We. 17 Alone. 19 Die. 21 Gypsy. 23 At. 24 Area. 26 Letter. 28 End. 29 Me. **(down)** 1 Fire. 2 Over. 3 Waif. 4 Am. 5 Mildewed. 6 Heart. 8 Oh. 10 Ashes. 11 Twenty. 14 Damsel. 15 Foe. 18 Nest. 20 Peat. 21 Glee. 22 Jet. 23 Arm. 25 An. 27 To.

10 **DATES** 1 November 5th. 2 March 1st. 3 May 5th. 4 August 10th. 5 June 1st. 6 January 19th. 7 January 3rd. 8 June 1st. 9 April 4th. 10 January 15th. **RELATIONS** 1 Matthewson. 2 Peggy. 3 Jonas. 4 Naomi. 5 Victor. 6 Edward. 7 Theodore. 8 Jessy. 9 Annabella. 10 Louisa.

11 **WORD SEARCH: PETS (across)** Carlo, Black Bess, Skulker, Throttler, Phoenix, Wolf. **(down)** Mesrour, Snap, Jack, Yorke, Sancho, Grey Tom, Grimalkin, Sylvie, Tartar, Juno. **(diagonal)** Minny, Fanny, Pilot, Prince, Dash, Ruby, Nimrod, Gnasher, Phoebe, Charlie, Zoe.

12 **NAME GAME 2** Mary Grey, Agnes Grey, Edward Weston, Mr Richardson, Rosalie Murray, Mr Hatfield, Sir Thomas Ashby, Mrs Bloomfield, John Murray, Charles Murray, Mr Robson, Mrs Murray, Nancy Brown. **(down)** Matilda Murray.

13 **FLOWERS** 1 Honeysuckle. 2 Forget-me-not. 3 Foxgloves. 4 Lilac. 5 Bluebells. 6 Primrose. 7 Crocus. 8 Violets. 9 Stocks and Wallflowers. 10 Orange trees, cacatuses, camellias, geraniums.

14 **ILLUSTRATION** Jane Eyre, Mr Brocklehurst, Mrs Reed.

15 **VILLETTE (across)** 1 Mists. 4 Maps. 7 Awe. 9 Rivers. 10 Cake. 12 Same. 14 No. 18 Fragrance. 20 Dark. 21 Chill. 22 Or. 24 Godmother. 26 Still. 27 As. 28 Row. **(down)** 1 Merit. 2 Seven. 3 Sort. 4 My. 5 Sake. 6 He. 8 We. 10 Capricious. 11 Am. 13 Steal. 15 Of. 16 Lace. 17 Scarlet. 19 Neither. 20 Do. 23 Doll. 25 Raw.

16 **NAME GAME 3** Mrs Pryor, Caroline Helstone, Robert Moore, Shirley Keeldar, Louis Moore, Harry Sympson, Hiram Yorke, Sir Philip Nunnely, Hortense Moore, Martin Yorke, Mr Helstone. **(down)** Peter Malone.

17 **CHRISTMAS** 1 Agnes Grey. 2 Ellen Dean. 3 La Terrasse. 4 St John Rivers. 5 1777. 6 Eliza and Georgiana Reed. 7 Wuthering Heights. 8 Helen Huntingdon. 9 One shilling. 10 Miss Marchmont.

18 **ILLUSTRATION** Gilbert Markham and Frederick Lawrence.

19 **AGNES GREY (across)** 1 Bookworm. 6 End. 8 Unruly. 9 Tracts. 11 Romp. 12 Learn. 13 Ocean. 15 Spy. 17 Solitude. 21 Us. 22 As. 24 One. 24 Emotion **(down)** 1 Bluebells. 2 Our. 3 Wilderness. 4 Metropolis. 5 Educate. 7 Unseen. 10 Heavy. 14 And. 16 Pies. 18 Last. 19 Upon. 20 Even. 21 Use.

20 **NAME GAME 4** Rachel, Lord Lowborough, Fergus Markham, Helen Huntingdon, Eliza Millward, Walter Hargrave, Esther Hargrave, Frederick Lawrence, Arthur Huntingdon, Mr Hattersley, Mrs Maxwell. **(down)** Rose Markham.

21 **CLOTHES** 1 Lowood pupils. 2 Rosalie Murray. 3 Zillah. 4 Edward Crimsworth. 5 Alfred de Hamal. 6 Mr Rochester. 7 Mme Beck. 8 Miss Temple. 9 Hortense Moore. 10 Arthur Huntingdon's puppy.

22 **ILLUSTRATION** Agnes Grey, Rosalie Murray and Mr Hatfield.

23 **JANE EYRE (across)** 1 Red-room. 5 Each. 7 All.
8 News. 9 Furs. 10 Dare. 11 To. 14 Governess. 17 Oh.
18 Bass. 20 Ivy. 21 Get. 22 Hit. 24 He. 25 She.
26 Human. 29 Iceberg. 30 Ten. 31 Won. **(down)**
1 Reader. 2 Do. 3 One. 4 Master. 5 Elf. 6 Curls. 8 Negus.
12 Or. 14 No. 15 Enigma. 16 Shy. 18 Bee. 19 At.
21 Ghost. 22 Herbs. 23 Thorn. 27 Noon. 28 Sin.

24 **COLOURS** 1 Crimson. 2 Blue. 3 Purple. 4 Indigo.
5 Lilac. 6 Pink. 7 White. 8 Auburn. 9 Green. 10 Brown.

ILLUSTRATION Lucy Snowe.

25 **WORD SEARCH: PUPILS (across)** Rosalie, Jane,
Charles, Isabelle, Mary Anne, Angelique, Harriet.
(down) Virginie, Julia, Dolores, Catherine, Helen,
Hortense, Sylvie, Leonie, Agnes, Matilda, Caroline,
Frances. **(diagonal)** Eulelie, Juanna, Jules, John, Adele,
Ginevra, Tom, Fanny, Aurelia, Blanche.

26 **NAME GAME 5** Alfred de Hamal, Madame Beck,
Ginevra Fanshawe, Pere Silas, Dr John, Polly Home,
Paul Emanuel, Mrs Bretton, Madame Walravens, Lucy
Snowe, Fifine Beck. **(down)** Desiree Beck.

27 **COOKERY** 1 Rose Markham. 2 Mutton Chops. 3 Red
Herrings. 4 Marmalade. 5 Pease. 6 Porridge. 7 A pair of
chickens. 8 Mrs Gale. 9 Marsh End. 10 Caroline Helstone.

28 **ILLUSTRATION** Shirley Keeldar and Joseph Donne.

29 **THE TENANT OF WILDFELL HALL (across)**
2 Westering. 6 As. 7 Flight. 8 Name. 9 Harm. 10 Me.
11 My. 12 Dried. 15 To. 16 Girl's. 17 Go. 18 Corn.
20 Expedition. 24 Bed. **(down)** 1 Painting. 2 Wife.
3 Spices. 4 Rather. 5 Gemmed. 11 Married. 12 Do.
13 Embryo. 13 Us. 15 Too. 17 Grey. 18 Cat. 19 Rob.
21 It. 22 Is. 23 No.

30 **NAME GAME 6** Catherine Earnshaw, Isabella Linton,
Mr Lockwood, Hareton Earnshaw, Linton Heathcliff,
Edgar Linton, Hindley Earnshaw, Heathcliff, Frances
Earnshaw. **(down)** Ellen Dean.

31 **SEASONS** 1 Spring. 2 Michaelmas. 3 Hay Lane.
4. Whitsuntide. 5 M. Paul. 6 Winter. 7 Black stoves.
8 Oats. 9 'Marmion'. 10. 'Marmion'.

32 **ILLUSTRATION** William Crimsworth and Zoraide Reuter.

33 **SHIRLEY (across)** 1 Labour. 5 Bad. 7 New. 9 Women. 10 Cough. 12 Lie. 13 Life. 14 Timid. 15 Keep. 18 Laughing. 21 Land. 22 And. 25 Giant. 27 Vexes. 28 Eager. **(down)** 1 Ladylike. 2 Brace. 3 Unjust. 4 Dew. 6 Danger. 8 World. 11 Homage. 16 Pledge. 17 Age. 19 Inn. 20 Care. 22 Ate. 23 Dog. 24 Far. 26 Is.

34 **OCCUPATIONS** 1 Opera-dancer. 2 Doctor. 3 Lace-mender. 4 M.P. 5 Bookseller. 6 Clothier. 7 Corn-factor. 8 Schoolteacher. 9 Clergyman. 10 Solicitor.

VILLAGES 1. Morton. 2 Horton. 3 Seacombe-cum-Scaife. 4 Whinbury. 5 Gimmerton. 6 Deepden. 7 Lindenhope. 8 Millcote. 9 Whitcross. 10 Briarfield.

35 **WORD SEARCH: SERVANTS (across)** Grace Poole, Sally, Barbara, Robert Leaven, Williamson, Alice Wood, Ellen Dean, Sophie, Hannah, Joseph, Manon, Louison, Eliza. **(down)** Fred Murgatroyd, Jenny, Goton, Martha Abbot, Benson, Brown, Trinette, Michael, Rosine, Warren. **(diagonal)** Fanny, Betty, Bessie Lee, Harriet, Zillah, Ruth, John, Sam, Mary.

36 **NAME GAME 7** Francois Pelet, Mr Seacombe, Zoraide Reuter, Jules Vanderkelkov, Edward Crimsworth, Caroline de Blemont, William Crimsworth, Yorke Hunsden, Lord Tynedale, Mrs King, Mr Brown, Victor Crimsworth. **(down)** Frances Henri.

37 **INTERIORS** 1 The studio at Wildfell Hall. 2 The kitchen at Marsh End. 3 Paulina's bedroom at the Hotel Crecy. 4 The dining room at Thornfield. 5 Catherine's bedroom at Wuthering Heights. 6 Edward Crimsworth's counting house. 7 The inn at the town of L--- between Gateshead and Lowood. 8 The parlour at 7 Faubourg Clotilde.

38 **ILLUSTRATION** Catherine Linton, Linton Heathcliff, Heathcliff and Ellen Dean.

39 **THE PROFESSOR (across)** 1 Penniless. 5 Peril. 7 Unique. 9 Literary. 11 Even. 14 Vile. 16 Am. 17 One. 18 Saw. 20 No. 22 Novice. 24 Tryste. 26 To. 28 On. 29 Widow. 30 Clerk. **(down)** 1 Pupil. 2 Nor. 3 Son. 4 Curve. 6 Lord. 7 Unromantic. 8 Is. 10 Talented. 12 Visit. 13 Name. 14 Void. 15 In. 16 As. 19 Woe. 21 Or. 23 Cook. 25 Yew. 27 He.

FRONT COVER ILLUSTRATION Jane Eyre

ABSON BOOKS

Other books in preparation in this Quiz and Puzzle series include:- Charles Dickens, William Shakespeare, Thomas Hardy, Mrs Gaskell and George Eliot.

Available now:-

THE JANE AUSTEN QUIZ AND PUZZLE BOOK
by Maggie Lane - £1.75

A variety of puzzles and quizzes designed to test your knowledge of the novels of Jane Austen. All the answers may be found in the six novels and are included in the back of the book.

AMERICAN ENGLISH/ENGLISH AMERICAN - 85p
A glossary of everday words which have completely different meanings depending upon which side of the Atlantic you happen to be.

RHYMING COCKNEY SLANG - 85p
A glossary to help you use your loaf (of bread - head) in getting about London.

SCOTTISH ENGLISH/ENGLISH SCOTTISH - 85p
A glossary of everyday Scottish words. Informative for newcomers and visitors - evocative for expatriates.

IRISH ENGLISH/ENGLISH IRISH - 85p
A glossary of words to help disentangle the delightful Irish gift of the gab. This includes a section on the vocabulary associated with *the troubles.*

AUSTRALIAN ENGLISH/ENGLISH AUSTRALIAN - 85p
A glossary of words helpful to all who journey to or from the world's largest island and smallest continent.

CB RADIO ENGLISH - 85p
A pocket glossary of CB Radio words and codes to enable you to take to the airwaves with speed and professionalism.

THE BRISTOL & BATH PUZZLER
by Richard Palmer - 50p

Fifteen crossword puzzles concerned with these two cities e.g. Famous Bristolians and Bathonians, TV., Street, Blankety Blank, Robins and Pirates, Pub Crawl, etc.

A full list of Abson books will be sent on request.

 All available from booksellers or by adding 15p for the first copy and 8p per copy thereafter for packing and postage from the publishers, Abson Books, Abson, Wick, Bristol BS15 5TT.